Sam at the Beach

Originally published as *Sam at the Seaside*

Written by **Mary Labatt**

Illustrated by **Marisol Sarrazin**

SCHOLASTIC INC.

New York Toronto London Auckland Sydney
Mexico City New Delhi Hong Kong Buenos Aires

Sam at the Beach
Originally published as *Sam at the Seaside*

No part of this publication may be reproduced, stored in a retrieval system,
or transmitted in any form or by any means, electronic, mechanical, photocopying,
recording, or otherwise, without written permission of the publisher. For
information regarding permission, write to Kids Can Press Ltd.,
29 Birch Avenue, Toronto, Ontario, Canada M4V 1E2.

ISBN-13: 978-0-545-14970-9
ISBN-10: 0-545-14970-3

Text copyright © 2006 by Mary Labatt.
Illustrations copyright © 2006 by Marisol Sarrazin. All rights reserved.
Published by Scholastic Inc., 557 Broadway, New York, NY 10012,
by arrangement with Kids Can Press Ltd. Kids Can Read is a registered trademark
of Kids Can Press Ltd. SCHOLASTIC and associated logos are trademarks and/or
registered trademarks of Scholastic Inc.

12 11 10 9 8 7 6 5 4 3 2 1   9 10 11 12 13 14/0

Printed in the U.S.A.   23

First Scholastic printing, May 2009

Designed by Marie Bartholomew

Joan and Bob were making sandwiches.

Bob made egg sandwiches.

Joan made peanut butter sandwiches.

"Yum!" thought Sam.

Joan got a big basket.

Bob put the sandwiches in the basket.

"Come on, Sam," said Joan.

"We are going to the seaside."

"What is the seaside?" thought Sam.

"Why does it need sandwiches?"

Joan and Bob got in the car.

Sam got in, too.

They drove out of town.

They drove past fields and farms.

Sam stuck her nose in the air.

She smelled something.

"Is that the seaside?" she thought.

"This is the seaside, Sam," said Joan.

Sam saw water and sand.

She saw seagulls and boats

and people and dogs.

"Wow!" thought Sam.

"I can have fun here!"

Joan and Bob sat on the blanket.

They ate sandwiches.

"Woof!" said Sam.

"Sandwiches are not for puppies,"

said Joan.

"Hmph," thought Sam.

"I need to have fun," thought Sam.

She ran to the water.

She walked in the water

just like the people.

Sam did not see a big wave coming.

SPLASH!

The wave hit Sam!

Sam saw some kids making a sandcastle.

"That looks like fun," she thought.

"I will do that."

Sam ran to the sandcastle.

She dug in the sand just like the kids.

She dug and dug.

Sam did not see where the sand was going.

"Stop puppy!" yelled the kids.

"Go away, puppy!"

Sam saw some crabs digging in the sand.

"That looks like fun," she thought.

"I will do that."

Sam ran to the crabs.

She put her nose down to sniff them.

Sam did not see a big crab coming.

The crab pinched Sam's nose.

"YOW!" said Sam.

Sam was wet and her nose hurt.

"I am having a bad time," she thought.

"I need to have fun."

Sam sat down.

"It is not fun to walk in the water.

It is not fun to make a sandcastle.

It is not fun to look at the crabs,"

she thought.

Then Sam saw a hot dog.

"Yum!" she thought.

"Awk!" said a seagull.

The seagull flew down

and grabbed the hot dog.

Sam saw an ice-cream cone.

"Yum!" she thought.

"Awk!" said a seagull.

The seagull flew down

and grabbed the cone.

"I am having a bad time," thought Sam.

"I do not like the seaside.

The seaside is not for puppies."

Then Sam saw something on the sand.

"Mmm," thought Sam.

"This is a good smell."

She poked the thing with her nose.

It did not move.

"Good," she thought.

"This thing will not bite me."

Sam sniffed and sniffed.

"Mmm-mmmm," she thought.

"I LOVE this smell!"

Sam rolled on the sand.

"Now I am having fun!" she thought.

"Oh, no!" yelled Joan.

"Oh, no!" yelled Bob.

"That is stinky!" yelled Joan.

"Stop, Sam! Stop!" yelled Bob.

Sam did not hear Joan and Bob.

She loved the fish smell.

She rolled and rolled.

"Awk!!" said a seagull.

He dived at Sam.

"AWK!!! AWK!!!

AWK!!! AWK!!!"

Sam ran to the blanket.

The seagull dived and dived.

Sam tried to hide under the blanket.

"Yikes!" yelled Joan.

"Yikes!" yelled Bob.

"You smell bad!" yelled Joan.

"Off the blanket!" yelled Bob.

Joan and Bob packed up.

They took the blanket.

They took the basket.

They held their noses.

"You stink, Sam," they said.

"I do not stink," thought Sam.

"I smell wonderful!"